LINDA HELLER

Alexis and the Golden Ring

MACMILLAN PUBLISHING CO., INC.
New York
COLLIER MACMILLAN PUBLISHERS
London

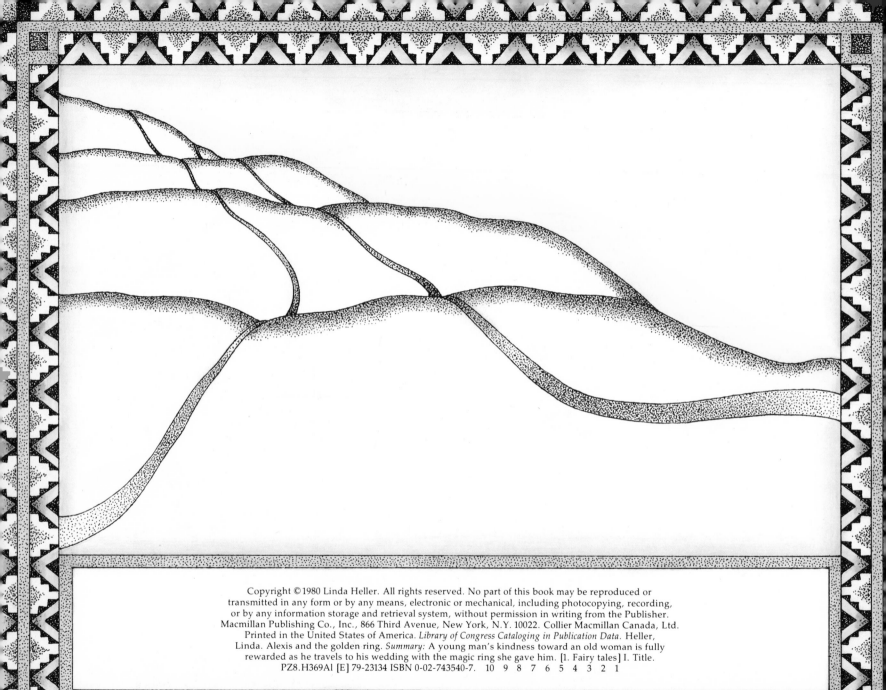

Macmillan Publishing Co., Inc., 866 Third Avenue, New York, N.Y. 10022. Collier Macmillan Canada, Ltd.
Printed in the United States of America. *Library of Congress Cataloging in Publication Data.* Heller,
Linda. Alexis and the golden ring. *Summary:* A young man's kindness toward an old woman is fully
rewarded as he travels to his wedding with the magic ring she gave him. [1. Fairy tales] I. Title.
PZ8.H369Al [E] 79-23134 ISBN 0-02-743540-7.   10 9 8 7 6 5 4 3 2 1

For my Aunt Sylvia and Aunt Etta

One Autumn long ago, when plump ripe pumpkins lay in the fields and the wheat had been cut and stacked and was ready for market, a young man named Alexis hurried down the road. His steps were light and he sang as he walked, hardly noticing the yellow and orange leaves that swirled about or the cows being driven home for winter. He was on his way to his wedding in the village of Pavlodar and could think only of his dear Natasha.

When Alexis had gone some distance, he saw an old woman bent low with heavy firewood, slowly crossing the field. Alexis ran to help her, thinking it would take only a few minutes. But the old woman lived far away, and it was dark when they reached her cottage.

As Alexis stored the branches near the fireplace, he spoke of Natasha. "Go to her, she will be worried," said the old woman. But Alexis could not bear to see her struggle with the heavy branches and stayed to help. When they finished, cold morning light pressed against the window.

"Hurry now, and please take some bread to eat along the way," said the old woman, opening her cupboard. Alexis saw that it was almost empty and thought, "How can I eat honey cake at my wedding while she has nothing?" He took her basket and went out into the fields.

The harvest was nearly over. Alexis searched field after field and found nothing. At last, far from the old woman's cottage, he found enough apples, cabbage and corn to fill her basket. Light snow fell as he returned.

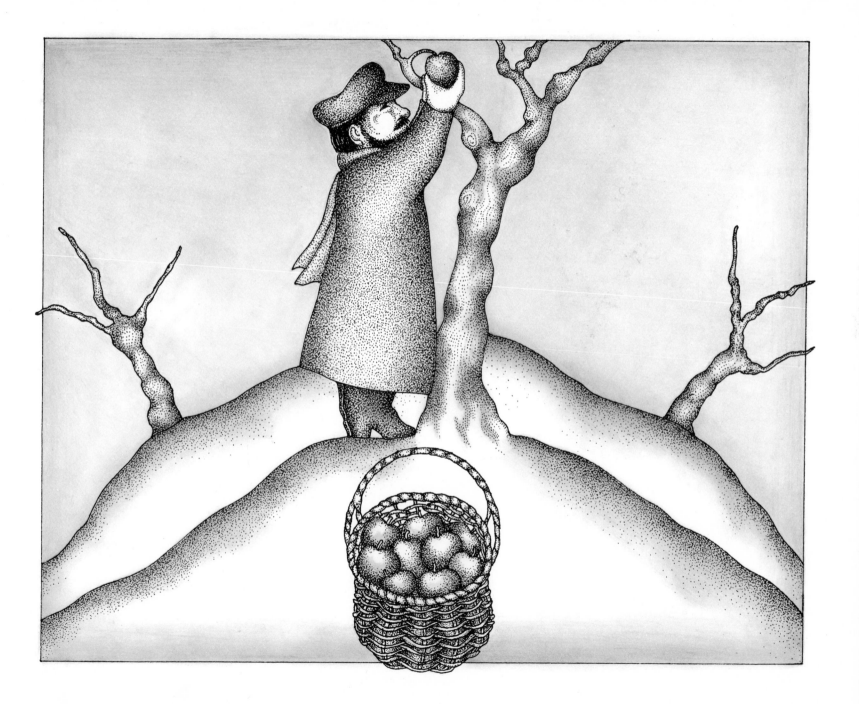

"I must go now," said Alexis. As he spoke, the winter wind roared and tried to enter the cottage, shaking the windows. It found cracks in the walls and slipped through. The old woman shivered. Alexis knew he must stay and repair the walls. Each time a crack was filled, the wind forced its way through a new one. The days passed, each shorter than the last. Slowly the house grew warm. The walls were mended. When Alexis looked through the window, deep snow covered the ground.

"Hurry now, Natasha will be worried," said the old woman, slipping a worn golden ring from her finger. "And take this. It will help you as you helped me." Alexis took the ring and thanked her. Then he hurried toward Pavlodar.

Wind swirled around Alexis and icy snow stung his face. He thought of Natasha and how worried she must be. He would give her the golden ring the moment he arrived. For safekeeping he put it on his finger. Suddenly the wind calmed and snow no longer fell. Alexis was surprised until he remembered the words of the old woman.

Soon Alexis came to a black, churning river. As he searched for a place to cross, he felt the ring pull his hand to the glistening snow. To his amazement he gathered the snow and shaped it into a fish.

The fish's round eyes grew dark, its body iridescent. Light passed through its snow fins, and they became thin and transparent. It spoke to Alexis in a strange fish voice, urging him to climb on its back. Then it slowly spread its fins and rose into the air. The fish carried Alexis safely to the other shore, grew pale, and turned again to snow.

Alexis hurried on. He came to a small hill and climbed it easily. When he reached the top, he stopped. Two huge bears stared up at him. Alexis moved slowly, careful not to anger them. But he slipped and began to somersault down the hill. The bears grew alarmed as Alexis rolled toward them. They growled and rose up on their hind legs. A giant paw struck Alexis, grazing his golden ring.

At once Alexis was back on his feet, whirling about in the arms of the bear. It held him gently as they danced to the music the other bear played on his small golden drum. When the dance was over, Alexis bowed to the bears and said good-by.

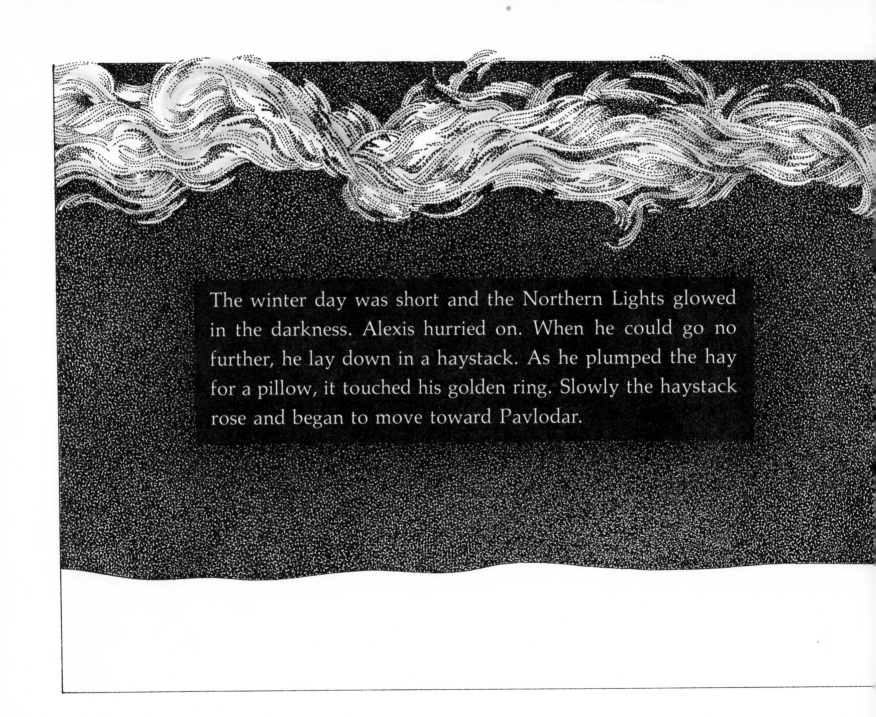

The winter day was short and the Northern Lights glowed in the darkness. Alexis hurried on. When he could go no further, he lay down in a haystack. As he plumped the hay for a pillow, it touched his golden ring. Slowly the haystack rose and began to move toward Pavlodar.

Alexis looked down and saw that the haystack had become a giant camel that swayed gently as it walked. Alexis lay back snug and warm to dream of Natasha. When he woke at dawn, the camel was once again a haystack. Alexis slid down and continued on his way.

Alexis was now at the foot of the mountains. Digging his boot into a crevice, he began to pull himself up to the first low peak. As his golden ring touched the jagged ice, the ice softened into warm fur.

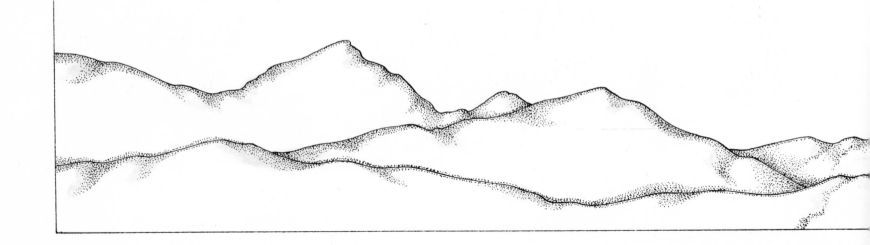

The mountain had become a herd of sleeping goats who woke when Alexis stroked them. They offered him their milk for breakfast. When Alexis sat on the back of the largest goat, he could see the entire countryside. Pavlodar was very close. He jumped down and ran to it.

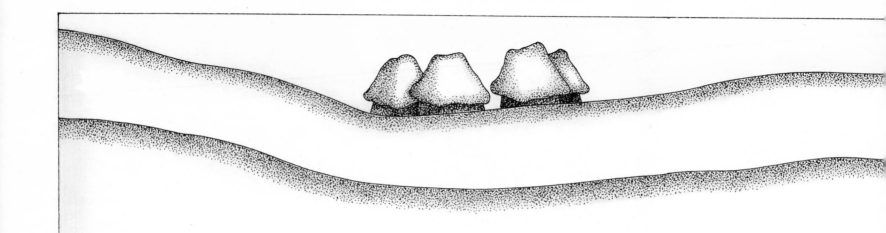

Alexis could see Natasha and the others. They stood at the edge of the village searching for him. Alexis was near, but they could not wave or run to him. Snowflakes covered their finely embroidered clothes. They had waited there since the day he was to arrive, long before, and had frozen in the cold. Alexis rushed to them.

As he slipped the golden ring on Natasha's icy finger, a wisp of white breath left her lips and her cheeks grew rosy. She greeted him joyfully.

Alexis and Natasha were married, and
they danced until the snow melted and
fine green leaves grew on the trees.